My Kitten

by
Margaret O'Hair

illustrated by
Tammie Lyon

Marshall Cavendish Children

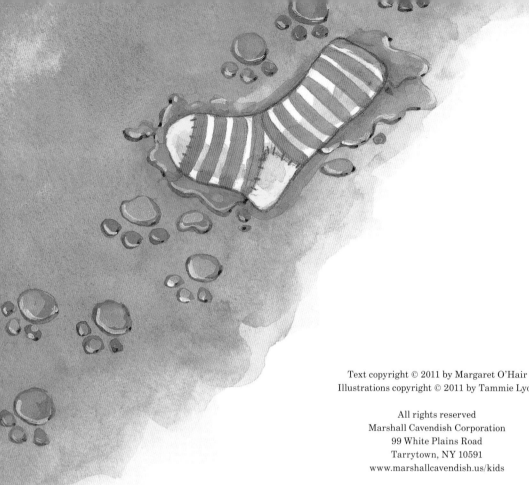

Marshall Cavendish Corporation
99 White Plains Road
Tarrytown, NY 10591
www.marshallcavendish.us/kids

Library of Congress Cataloging-in-Publication Data
O'Hair, Margaret.
My kitten / by Margaret O'Hair ; illustrated by Tammie
Lyon. — 1st ed.
p. cm.
Summary: Brief rhyming text and illustrations show a
kitten's activities, from dreaming in the sunlight to playing
with a ball of yarn.
ISBN 978-0-7614-5811-1
[1. Stories in rhyme. 2. Cats—Fiction. 3. Animals—
Infancy—Fiction.] I. Lyon, Tammie, ill. II. Title.
PZ8.3.O353Mxk 2011   [E]—dc22   2009052902

The illustrations were rendered in gouache and color pencil.
Book design by Vera Soki
Editor: Robin Benjamin
Printed in China (E)
First edition
10 9 8 7 6 5 4 3 2 1

For Sam and Stephanie
—M.O'H.

For the kids at Montague Elementary School,
especially Keelan and Irelyn Lyon
—T.L.

Dream kitten,
fluff kitten,
sun kitten,
light.

Yawn kitten,
stretch kitten,
sweet kitten,
bright.

Food kitten,
munch kitten,
yum kitten,
eat.

Lick kitten,
fur kitten,
clean kitten,
neat.

Bowl kitten,
gold kitten,
fish kitten,
stare.

Scoot kitten,
leap kitten,
jump kitten,
chair.

"No, kitten, don't, kitten, stop, kitten, claws."

"Yes, kitten,
good, kitten,
nice, kitten,
paws."

Ball kitten,
roll kitten,
yarn kitten,
bounce.

String kitten,
swipe kitten,

spring kitten,
pounce.

Door kitten,
out kitten,
squirrel kitten,
see.

Grass kitten,
leaves kitten,

climb kitten,
tree.

"Here, kitten,
come, kitten,

cute kitten,
hug."

Hold kitten,
my kitten,
soft kitten,
snug.

"Here, kitten,
dish, kitten,
drink, kitten,
cream."

Blink kitten,
purr kitten,
sleep kitten,
dream.